Who's That Girl?

Palmetto Publishing Group
Charleston, SC

Who's That Girl?
Copyright © 2020 by Natasha Gatewood
All rights reserved

No portion of this book may be reproduced, stored in a retrieval system, or transmitted in any form by any means–electronic, mechanical, photocopy, recording, or other except for brief quotations in printed reviews, without prior permission of the author.

First Edition

Printed in the United States

Paperback: 978-1-64990-128-6
eBook: 978-1-64990-127-9

Who's That Girl?

Natasha Gatewood

It was the first day back from spring break, and all the students were so excited to see each other.

"Hi, Jason."

"What's up, gnarly Karly?"

"Hey, Kennedi."

"Hi, Kim."

"OK, class, settle down; let's all sit down," said Ms. McClain. Ms. McClain was the teacher to the smartest class in sixth grade. They were like one big family; after all they had all been friends since kindergarten.

"Good morning, class, and welcome back," said Ms. McClain. "Everyone had a great spring break I hope."

"Awesome," said Adam.

"Mine was boring, boring, and more boring," said Elijah.

"What about you, Bianca?" asked Kim.

"Yeah, how was it?" said Karly. Everyone turned with excitement just to hear her answer.

"It was awesome," said Bianca.

"OK, class," said Ms. McClain, "how about we get started by everyone coming up and giving us a brief oral report on how you spent your spring break." She added, "Let's start with you, Mr. Boring," as she turned to Elijah.

"Ha ha ha," everyone laughed.

"And she said brief, Elijah!" yelled Karly. Everyone knew Elijah would start to talk and go on and on for hours.

"Well, all I did was babysit my little brother, who was a handful. I cut the grass, for the first time ever, which took forever, and our yard is not even that big. I washed the car; with as long as it took, it felt like I was washing a whole bus. And I did chores every single day. Just awful, I tell you. Awful!" shouted Elijah. "Can you believe she made me wash the walls and windows?"

"Elijah!" yelled Karly. "She said brief!"

"Well that was it," said Elijah.

"Jeez, no fun kid stuff," whispered Adam.

"So sorry to hear that Elijah; well hopefully your summer break will be better," said Ms. McClain. "OK, who'd like to go next?" she asked.

The students began beating on their desks, shouting, "Bianca, Bianca, Bianca!"

"OK, OK, if you insist," said Bianca in an arrogant voice. All the students loved Bianca; after all she was the smartest and one of the cutest girls in the class. She had always been the leader of the group. They called her the queen bee. When the teacher asked a question, they wouldn't even raise their hands to answer until Bianca raised hers first. They all would wait to see what she'd say first before even attempting to answer a question. Not to mention her mom always brought chips and juice for the class on Tuesdays and cupcakes on Fridays. And she also threw the best birthday parties.

"Well, I had a terrific spring break, unlike others," said Bianca while glancing at Elijah. "My family went to Disney World. I got to swim with dolphins, and I even got to lead the annual Disney princess parade."

"Oh, wow!" everyone cried out.

"Only movie stars get to lead that!" exclaimed Kennedi.

"You always have the best spring breaks ever," said Ethan. Bianca walked back to her seat knowing she still held the title "spring break queen."

"No one can top that," she thought in her head.

"OK, who is next?" asked Ms. McClain. Everyone shamefully put their heads down, fearing their story would not be as good as Bianca's. "No one?" asked Ms. McClain. "Well I'll tell my story," she said. "I got to clean all the cat hair and fur balls out of my sink; I permed my dog Lester's hair and even got to paint my parrot blue."

"Ha ha ha," giggled all the kids. After hearing her funny story, they slowly got the courage to share their stories.

As Benny got up to tell his story, Nathan yelled out, "OMG, what's that smell!"

"Oh that? Oh that's my new cologne I made over the break. I call it Benny Berry."

"It smells more like gym socks and rotten eggs berry," said Kennedi.

"Well we already know what you did over your break," said Mrs. McClain.

"Yeah, lost his sense of smell," said Kennedi. The entire class, even Benny, burst out in laughter.

"As a matter of fact," said Benny, "yes, I made all different kinds of cologne."

"And that's the one he chose to wear?" whispered Kennedy.

"I made Benny Berry, Benny Banana, and Benny Fruity Berry; the fruity is for the girls." He smiled and winked. "I call it the Benny Collection."

"OMG, who's next?" asked Kennedi, rolling her eyes.

"OK, Benny, glad you found your creative side during the break," said Ms. McClain. "Now let's move on." The other kids all told their spring break stories, but none compared to Bianca's. After they heard the last story, it was time for recess. "Single file line," said Ms. McClain.

"I'm 'bout to shoot so many threes they going to think I'm Steph Curry," said Adam.

"Smells like Benny's already been outside shooting threes," said Kennedi laughing. The girls ran off to do their usual jump rope contest, and all the boys ran to the basketball court.

As the girls were jumping rope, they sang, "Miss Mary Mack, Mack, Mack. All dressed in black, black, black. With silver buttons, buttons, buttons. All down her back, back, back." Suddenly Kim stopped singing, and her jaw dropped.

"What are you doing, Kim?" Bianca yelled.

"Look! Who is that?" asked Kim. All the girls' heads turned. All the boys stopped playing basketball to look. Their mouths flew wide open.

"Wow! Who is that?" asked Elijah with his eyes wide.

"Man, she's pretty," said Adam.

"Sure is!" hollered Benny.

Ms. McClain walked up with a new girl. "OK, everyone, this is our new student, Jasmine," she stated. The girls were not so thrilled.

Jasmine had long silky hair and smooth caramel-toned skin. "She looks like a real-life Barbie doll," said Kim. The girls just stared at her.

"She looks like an angel," said Adam.

Bianca felt something she had never felt before and instantly went into mean-girl mode. Bianca told her friends, "Hey, girls, watch this." Pretending to be friendly, she went over to Jasmine. "Hi, how are you? I'm Bianca. Do you want to come jump rope with us?"

"Sure," said Jasmine.

"Let's double Dutch," said Kim.

"OK, Jasmine, you and Kennedi jump in," said Bianca. As jasmine got ready to jump in, Bianca winked at Kim. "*Wakow!*"

"Ouch!" screamed Jasmine.

"*Oh no*! I'm sorry. The rope must have slipped out of my hand," said Bianca, in a sarcastic voice. "Are you OK?"

"Yeah, I'm fine," said Jasmine. "It's OK."

"OK, class, let's go in," said Ms. McClain. "Jasmine you can have the empty desk by Bianca," said the teacher.

"Oh great," said Bianca, pretending to be happy as she rolled her eyes.

"Well, Jasmine, at the start of class everyone was telling about their spring break. How about you come and tell us a little about yourself and your spring break," said Ms. McClain. As Jasmine walked to the front, all the boys' heads raised up in attention, and the girls' noses turned up just the same.

"Hi, my name is Jasmine, but everyone calls me Jazz. My dad is in the army, so we move around a lot. I last lived in Hawaii. I spent my spring break hiking mountains, I went to the volcano park and rode a Jet Ski in the Pacific Ocean," stated Jasmine.

"Oh my gosh!" shouted Adam. "All of the students, except Bianca, were so impressed and excited to hear more."

"Did you see any bears while you were hiking?" asked Benny.

"Nooo, there aren't any bears in Hawaii. The closest you come to a wild animal is a pig, which I did see, and I even got a picture. We made sure not to get too close, but it still spotted us and started to chase us. Can you believe I got chased by a wild pig?" she answered.

The students gasped. "Wow!"

"But my dad distracted him by throwing an apple while we ran into a cave until the park ranger came, but I'm used to it. We do that all the time," said Jazz. "But yeah, that was my spring break. Nothing special."

Even Ms. McClain was impressed. "Well I think that was by far the most interesting spring break story we've heard today," said Ms. McClain.

"Yes, yes," screamed all the students in agreement. Kennedi and Kim slid their desks closer to Jazz. So did Adam.

"Hey, let me into the group too," said Adam. "Hi, I'm Adam. I'm the star of the basketball team and also the star of your life," said Adam in his cool voice to Jasmine.

"Well nice to meet you, Adam" said Jasmine, trying to hold back her laughter.

"But can I ask you a question?" asked Adam.

"Sure," said Jasmine.

"Are you from Tennessee? 'Cause you're the only ten I see," said Adam.

"Oh wow, you sure do have a lot of pickup lines" she said laughing. "But no, I guess you could say I'm from everywhere as much as I have moved around.

"So, have you ever lived in California?" asked Kennedi.

"Of course," said Jazz.

"Oh wow, did you meet any movie stars? Not really. Just the entire cast of *Black-ish and Stranger Things*.

"Aah," sighed Kim. "I think I'm going to faint. Where did you meet them at?"

"The Kids' Choice Awards," she said.

"*The Kids' Choice Awards!*" shouted Kennedi.

"Hey, what's going on over there? Quiet down," said Ms. McClain.

"But, Ms. McClain, she said she went to the Kids' Choice Awards. Do you know how big of a deal that is?" asked Kennedi.

"Yeah, that's better than eating ice cream for dinner for the rest of my life," said Ethan.

"OK, class, let's settle down and get to work," said Ms. McClain.

"You're, like, famous," whispered Kennedi to Jazz.

That really made Bianca's blood boil. She felt her number one spot slipping away. "Oh, I'll give her an interesting story to tell," Bianca thought to herself.

As the students headed out for lunch, Bianca was plotting her plan in her head. All the girls were sitting at their favorite lunch table. "Hey, Jazz, come sit with us!" shouted Bianca.

"OK!" Jasmine said with excitement. She was happy to make new friends on her first day. On her way over, Bianca slid her leg out and tripped her. Food went flying everywhere. All the kids laughed.

"OMG, what happened?" cried out Bianca, with a surprised but sneaky look on her face.

Jasmine was so embarrassed. She ran to the bathroom and cried. Kennedi ran to check on her. "Are you OK?"

"Yeah, I just slipped I guess," said Jazz. "I'll be OK."

The next morning Jazz came into the classroom with invitations. "What are those?" asked Kennedi.

"My mom's having a "welcome to the neighborhood" party to get to meet all of our new neighbors. She said I could invite my new classmates so we could get to know each other better."

"Oh, that sounds cool," said Kennedi. "Hey, everyone, Jazz is inviting us to a party this weekend." All the kids cheered.

"That's so cool," said Benny.

"You just make sure you don't wear your famous Benny Berry cologne," said Kennedi.

"Benny Berry, what's that?" giggled Jazz.

"What's that!" yelled Kennedi. "Do you have a nose?"

Jazz, laughing, said, "Oh, is that what I've been smelling all this time? I thought someone just forgot to change their socks for a week." All the girls laughed.

"Oh, don't pay Kennedi any mind," said Benny.

"I don't believe this, so now she's trying to steal all my friends too," thought Bianca to herself. "OK, game on!" Bianca kept quiet the rest of the morning, thinking and plotting of ways to get at Jasmine and anyone else that stood in her way of being number one.

Walking into school the next morning, Bianca was all ready to set her plan into motion. "It's about to go down," said Bianca to herself. "Hey, Kennedi, can I talk to you for a second," she said.

"Hey, Bianca, what's up?"

"You're one of my best friends, so I thought you should know that Jazz has been going around talking about you."

"Nooo, I don't believe that. She's so nice," said Kennedi.

"Sorry, friend, but it's true. She told me that you are so loud and nosey. She thinks you are jealous of her and want to be her. She said she can tell because you're always staring at her."

"Why that little roach!" shouted Kennedi. "I'm going to get her straight right now."

"No, no," said Bianca, "then she may want to fight. If I were you, I'd let it go and not talk to her anymore. Silence and not being her friend will hurt worse than your words."

"Maybe you're right," replied Kennedi.

"Haven't I always been?" asked Bianca.

"You're such a good friend," said Kennedi.

"I know," replied Bianca, although part of her was feeling bad for telling a fib.

"No time for feelings right now," said a little voice in Bianca's head.

"Right," she said to herself. "OK, who's next. Hey, Benny, can I talk to you for a second?"

"Hey, queen bee, what's going on?" asked Benny.

"Well," she said, "I just thought you should know that the new girl, Jazz, has been telling everyone that you and Elijah are so creepy and even tried to follow her home yesterday."

"What!" yelled Benny.

"Yeah, she even said you told her that you invented the cologne so you can just spray it on everyday instead of taking baths," said Bianca.

"Why that little storyteller. I'm going to spray her right now!" shouted Benny.

"No, no," said Bianca, "then she may want to fight."

"If I were you, I'd let it go and not talk to her anymore. Ignoring her will hurt worse than your words," said Bianca.

"Good idea. Thanks for looking out," said Benny.

"No problem. What are friends for?" she whispered in his ear. Benny told Elijah what Bianca had said, so they decided to hold a meeting with the rest of the boys in the class. They all agreed to stay away from Jazz because she was clearly a troublemaker.

"Karly, Kim, have you heard what everyone's been saying?" asked Bianca.

"No, what?" they asked.

"Rumor has it that Jazz is saying you two are like Dumb and Dumber. She said you two can't even go to the bathroom without one another. She said that Kim follows behind you, Karly, like she's your little puppy dog and that you two could never be her real friends."

"Why that little wannabe diva," said Kim.

"If I were you, I'd let it go and not talk to her anymore. Silence will hurt worse than your words. Then she'd wish she had friends like you two," said Bianca.

"OMG, I love it, B!" said Karly. "You always know what to do."

"No problem. That's what friends are for," she said with an evil grin.

The bell rang, and everyone dashed to the classroom. "Hi, you guys," said Jazz. Everyone just looked at her with a nasty look. "Um, what's that all about?" thought Jazz in her head. No one talked to her the whole day. This went on for days. Jazz couldn't figure it out. "What did I do wrong?" she thought.

After class Bianca even went so far as to include Ms. McClain in her plan. As she walked by Ms. McClain's desk, she dropped a piece of paper on the floor. As Ms. McClain was cleaning the room, she noticed the paper. "Um, what's this?" she wondered. She picked it up and read it. She could not believe her eyes. It said, "Hey, Bianca, don't you think Ms. McClain's class is so boring and her jokes are so corny. All she talks about is her stinky cats. She's like the old cat lady who lived in a shoe. And don't let me get started on her hair. Oh my gosh, it looks like a fur ball. She probably has some cats hidden in there. Maybe we should hide a stray cat in her desk drawer, since she loves them so much, to jump out and scare her in the morning, LOL. If you agree check yes or no." It was signed "Jazz."

There was a check mark beside the "no." Bianca tried to make it seem that she did not agree with Jazz, although she was the one who really wrote this note. This would make Ms. McClain like Bianca even more.

The next morning Ms. McClain really had her eye on Jasmine. "OK, class, today we're going to work in groups with the boys versus girls to play a reading memory game," said Ms. McClain. All the girls had to sit at the table together. Of course, Karly and Kim sat beside each other. Jazz thought, "This is my time to break the ice," since no one had been talking to her. She said jokingly to Kim and Karly, "Wow, are you sure you two aren't really twins? Because you're always together." She laughed. Now this really made it look like what Bianca said was true. The girls just looked at her in shock, without even a little bit of a smile. Jazz didn't get why suddenly no one would talk to her. She had no idea of the stories Bianca had planted in everyone's minds.

"Hey, Kennedi, why are you so quiet?" asked Jazz. "That's not like you."

"So, what are you trying to say?" asked Kennedi. "I'm such a big mouth you think I don't know how to be quiet unless something is wrong."

"No, of course not," said Jazz. "I was just making sure you were OK."

"Yeah, right," said Kennedi while rolling her eyes. Waving her hand, she shouted, "Ms. McClain!"

"Yes, Kennedi," she replied.

"Do we have any Raid bug spray? I think I saw a talking roach," said Kennedi. All of the kids burst out into laughter.

Even Ms. McClain giggled. "No, we have no Raid or talking roaches."

Jazz was laughing until she realized the joke was about her. She decided it would be better not to say anything else. Bianca glowed with happiness when she saw her plan was working just the way she wanted. When lunch time came, Jazz just sat alone at the lunch table and softly whispered to herself, "I wish I could go back to my old school."

Of course, Bianca heard her and thought, "I wish you could too. Now let's make it happen."

Walking back to class after a lonely lunch, Jazz felt a quick push from behind. Karly, Kim, and Kennedi had tiptoed up from behind and pushed her in the janitor's closet. "No, no!" yelled Jazz, but the rest of the class had already gone ahead. The girls locked the door from the outside and ran off to class. Beating on the door, Jazz screamed for help, but no one could hear because all classes were back in session.

Luckily for her, it was time for the janitor to do his hourly rounds. As he approached the door, he could hear the pounding and screaming. He grabbed his broom like a sword because he was afraid also. "Who's there?" he asked.

"It's me, Jasmine Green. Help me, please!" she cried out. The janitor unlocked the door, and Jazz ran out crying. She ran straight to class, huffing and puffing.

"Jasmine, where have you been?" asked Ms. McClain.

"Someone pushed me in the janitor's closet and locked me in."

"Now, Jasmine, who would do a thing like that?" asked Ms. McClain.

"But Ms.---" Jazz tried to explain.

"No, young lady, just tell the truth. You were goofing off, and now you're late for class, so have a seat right now," said Ms. McClain with an attitude.

"I can't believe this is happening," mumbled Jazz to herself.

"Are you talking back?" asked Ms. McClain.

"Of course not!" yelled Jazz.

"Oh, so now you're yelling at me," said the teacher. "I've had about enough of you, young lady. You will be staying after school with the cat lady for detention," said Ms. McClain.

"I can't believe this is happening," thought Jazz. Once Jasmine made it home, she told her mom what had happened. "I hate that school!" she yelled.

"Oh, Jasmine," her mom said. "I'm sure it's not that bad."

"But, mom, it is. The kids never like the new girl, and that is -always me! I'm sick of us moving so much."

"Well, Jazzy," said her mom, "hopefully this will be our last time, and remember those who didn't like you in the beginning always ended up being your friends in the end. Now didn't they? So, I'm sure this time will be the same way."

"Whatever, mom. Ugh, parents just don't understand," Jasmine mumbled.

The next morning Bianca was so tired and sleepy from being up all night, thinking of new ways to get Jazz. She walked into the classroom like a zombie. "Oh my, Bianca, you look like a hot mess. Your hair looks like you stuck your finger in a socket," said Benny.

"Yeah, I wanted to look like you today, so I see its working," said Bianca. The class laughed. Bianca decided it was her time to get the ball rolling. "So, Jazz, is your mom still having her party Saturday?" asked Bianca.

"Yeah!" said Jazz with excitement. She was just so happy that someone, anyone, was talking to her again. "Are you guys coming?" she asked.

As all the girls looked at each other and where about to say no.

"Of course we are!" shouted Bianca. Her crew stared at her in disbelief.

"What in the world?" asked Karly.

"What's the start time again?" asked Bianca.

"Two p.m.," said Jazz. "We are having bouncy houses, waterslides, and clowns."

"Clowns?" asked Benny. "What are we, five years old?"

"No, silly, they're for my little brother and his friends." She giggled.

"Can we bring our bikes with us?" asked Bianca.

"Of course you can," she said.

"I can't wait. It's going to be so much fun," said Bianca. The other girls could not believe their ears.

"What is she doing?" said Kim to Karly.

"Beats me," said Karly.

After school Bianca called a special meeting with her friends. She explained to them that of course she is not excited about going to Jazz's party, but this is a great time for them to get their revenge for her talking about them behind their backs. "Great idea, Bianca. We should have known you were up to something," said Kennedi.

"Yeah, you're so smart," said Kim.

"What are friends for?" asked Bianca, with her evil grin. "Now here's the plan," she whispered.

It was Saturday morning, and the day of the party had finally arrived. Bianca woke up bright and early. She called each person in her crew to make sure everyone remembered what part they are supposed to be playing. All the girls lived on the same block, so they agreed to meet at Bianca's house first, at 3:00 p.m. sharp. "Is everyone in line?" shouted Bianca. "OK, it's 3:01. Let's roll out." The girls began riding their bikes down the street. They came upon Jazz's house and saw her sitting on the porch all alone.

"Hey, Jazz, we're here," yelled the girls.

Jazz jumped up off the porch with excitement. "Hi, you guys, I've been waiting for you," she said. "I thought you weren't coming. There's no one here but old people and little kids and, oh yeah, the berry boy, Benny." They all laughed.

"Well we're here now, so let's get this party started," said Kennedi.

"Let's go change our clothes so we can get on the waterslide," said the girls.

"Do you have the oil?" Bianca asked Karly.

"Yeah," she said.

"Hey, I'm going first!" yelled Kennedi. "Jazz, your last because you're the host," she said.

Each of the girls took turns sliding down the slide. When it was Jazz's turn, Kim distracted her so Karly could pour the oil on the slide. "Come on Jazz what are you waiting for!" yelled Karly.

"Here I come," she yelled back. Jazz ran and slid down the slide, but she couldn't stop. "Aah!" she screamed, as she slid right on into the bushes.

"OMG, are you OK?" Kim asked as the girls looked on and laughed.

"Yeah, I'm fine," said Jazz. "I just don't understand why I couldn't stop. Everyone else stopped."

"Who knows," said Bianca. "But hey, you're OK, so let's go play pin the tail on the donkey."

"OK, let me grab a T-shirt first," said Jazz.

"Ready, girls?" Bianca asked her crew.

"Yeah," they replied devilishly.

"Hey, Jazz, you can go first," said Kennedi.

"Yeah, since it seems like going last is bad luck for you," chuckled Karly.

"OK, cool beans," said Jazz. They blindfolded her and spun her around.

"Are you dizzy yet?" asked Bianca.

"Gosh yeah," she said.

"OK, go." Jazz felt her way around, feeling nothing but space and air.

"You're getting warmer," said Bianca.

The girls began chanting. "Jasmine! Jasmine! Jasmine! Keep going; you're getting closer," they all hollered out. "You're almost there." Next all you could hear was howling.

"Woof! Woof!" the dog was barking.

"OMG, Jazz, you pinned the tail on the neighbor's dog," said Karly. Jazz took off the blindfold, screamed, and took off running. The dog took off behind her. It chased her all around the yard.

"*Help*!" screamed Jazz as she ran, trying to dodge the guest.

"I'll save you!" yelled Benny.

"Oh sit down somewhere, Benny," thought Bianca, so she tripped him. Benny went tumbling down to the ground. Jazz finally came to a stop when she fell over a chair and face first into the cake on the table.

The girls ran over to her. "Jazz, are you OK?" they asked.

"Aah," Jazz sighed. "Never been better," she said sarcastically and laughed. Everyone couldn't help but laugh with her.

"OK, let's get you cleaned up," said her mom. When Jazz came back out, everyone was dancing and having a good time.

"Hey, Jazz, let's go for a ride," said Kim.

"Yeah, I want to feel the wind blow through my hair," said Karly.

"Well I just want to get away from all of these old folks," said Kennedi.

"I know, right?" said the girls while laughing. Jazz grabbed her bike and joined them. They began riding around their block. Jazz noticed the girls turning the corner off their street.

"Where are we going?" asked Jazz.

"Oh, it's just a shortcut back to your house," said Karly. All of a sudden, the girls zoomed off, leaving Jazz in the dust.

"Wait up, you guys!" yelled Jazz. Bianca and the girls quickly turned another corner, leaving Jazz in their dust and not knowing which way she should go. She turned around, but being new to the neighborhood, she did not know which turns to take. After riding in circles for an hour, Jazz finally stopped and asked a lady who was working in her yard which way to get back to her street.

"Oh, sweetie, you're just right around the corner from here," said the lady. After getting directions Jazz rode back home alone, feeling sad. By now the party was over.

"Where have you been, Jazz?" asked her mom. "I was getting worried about you."

"I'm sorry, mom. I just went for a ride with my friends. I think I'm going to head to bed now, because I'm a little tired," said Jazz.

"Yeah, it's been a long day," said her mom.

"You have no idea," thought Jazz to herself.

On Monday at school, Jazz saw the girls for the first time since the party. "Hey, you guys left me," she said.

"Well it's not our fault you couldn't keep up, slow bunny," said Bianca as they all laughed and walked away. As Jazz walked into the classroom, she heard the girls still giggling. She just could not take it anymore.

"You girls are so fake and evil!" yelled Jazz. "I've never met such a wicked group of jealous girls in my life."

"I know she didn't call us jealous," said Kennedi.

"Why you wanna be—"

"No, hold up, Kennedi," said Bianca. "I got this one." Bianca stood up bold and tall. She leaned over Jasmine's desk and stared her directly in her eyes and said, "First of all, crybaby Jasmine, no one is jealous of you. You came here thinking you're all that and a bag of chips, telling your little hot-shot stories about Hawaii and Hollywood. No one believed you anyway. Then you think your hair is so pretty and long when really it looks like strings on a wet mop. You are so skinny you walk around here looking like a broomstick with teeth. You're so light you probably glow in the dark. You are jealous of us. That is why you talked about all my friends behind their back."

"No, I did not!" yelled Jazz.

"Yes you did, you glow worm!" yelled back Kennedi.

"You're just mad because we won't let you be a part of our crew. Oh, poor Jasmine, the lonely drifter. Well drift on away from here because nobody likes you," said Bianca.

"Well I never liked you either," said Jazz. "That's impossible because everyone likes me," said Bianca sarcastically with a smirk on her face. Ms. McClain walked into the room but only heard Jasmine's comment.

"Wait one minute. What's going on here?" shouted Ms. McClain.

"It's Jasmine," said Bianca. "She just started name calling and arguing with everyone. She even talked about you, Ms. McClain. All we were trying to do is be her friend."

"Why you storyteller!" yelled Jazz.

"Hey watch your mouth," said Ms. McClain. "I found your little letter, Jasmine, so I'm sure Bianca's not fibbing."

"What letter?" yelled Jazz. "This whole school is crazy!" she hollered.

"No, you're crazy!" yelled back Bianca. The two girls were shouting so loud other teachers began coming out of their classrooms just to see what was going on.

"I've had about enough of this!" yelled Ms. McClain. "Both of you report to the principal's office right now!"

"Now look what you've done, troublemaker," said Bianca to Jasmine. The two girls marched to the office. Ms. McClain told the principal what went on.

"I am really surprised at you Bianca," said Principal Johnson. "I think you two need a day off to think about what you have done, so I'm suspending both of you for one day," said the principal. "You also have to bring a parent back for a parent conference."

"Nooo," whimpered Jasmine. Bianca couldn't believe it. She had never been in trouble. The shock immediately took over her, and she suddenly fainted and fell out the chair.

"Oh my gosh!" yelled Ms. McClain. "Hurry, go get the nurse!"

"Wow, I didn't expect her to take it that hard," said Principal Johnson.

Once Bianca made it home, she had to explain to her mom what happened. Her mom couldn't believe what she was hearing. "Bianca," she said with disappointment, "you should be ashamed. I did not raise you to fight with others."

"I wasn't fighting. It was just a little argument, mom," said Bianca.

"Arguing and fighting are both the same in my book," said her mom. "I've never had any problems with you. What has gotten into you?" she asked.

"You just don't get it," sobbed Bianca. "She thinks she so pretty and perfect with her long silky hair and bright skin with no spots and no pimples. "She's just perfect." All the boys like her, and she's trying to steal my friends and my shine as top student," said Bianca in a deep mean voice. "Your shine?" asked her mom. "There's enough shine for everyone to go around."

"If only my hair could be long and pretty like hers," said Bianca. "And why did you have to make me so dark skinned!" she cried out. Her mom chuckled for a moment. "What's so funny?" asked Bianca.

"Oh nothing. It's just I remember those days," said her mom.

"Huh?" said Bianca, looking confused.

"First of all, I didn't make you that brown," she laughed. "God did." She began to tell her the story of when she was her age. "When I was around your age, I felt the same way. All the light-skinned girls with the long hair got all the attention. So one summer I prayed every night before bed, asking God to let me wake up with light skin and long hair before summer break was over. I'd wake up every morning and run to the mirror only to find myself still looking the same. I tried to make deals with God and even made promises to him about things he and I knew I couldn't fulfill."

"Promises like what?" asked Bianca.

"Oh, just things like, 'If you give me long pretty hair, I promise I won't ask for anything else for the rest of my life.' Or 'If you make my skin lighter, I promise not to eat chocolate ever again,' and you knooooow how I love chocolate."

"Oh wow!" said Bianca while laughing. "Yeah, you do love your chocolate. I can't believe you did that mom!"

"Yep, I did it," said her mom. "And at the end of summer I still couldn't understand why God didn't answer my prayers."

"What did grandma say?" asked Bianca.

"I never even told grandma. I have never told anyone until now. So, I guess we can say you are officially the first one to know about my secret struggles as a child," said her mom.

"Oh, am I supposed to feel special because of that?" asked Bianca in an arrogant voice.

"Listen here, smarty," said her mom, "there's a lesson to be learned from this. In the long run, I learned God didn't change my looks because he made me the way he wanted me to be. He makes everyone special in their own special way, even you. We are all different in some way. That is what makes you unique. Just like you want to be lighter skinned, there is some girl out there somewhere wishing she were darker or more tanned. Just like you are always complaining about being taller than your classmates, there is some girl out there wishing she could grow and be your height. Learn to be happy with the body you are blessed with. Never compare yourself to others. We are all one of a kind. God made you with your own unique talents and gifts. When you compare yourself to others, you only hurt yourself. You are too busy worrying about what another person has or is doing instead of focusing on the good in you. You must learn to love who you are, flaws and all. There may be features you have and do not like, but someone else may see them as great. None of us are perfect, and we all find flaws with ourselves. But always remember, baby girl, you are an original masterpiece, and no one can take that from you. I am a queen, and you are my princess. In my opinion, all women and girls are queens and little princesses. When you are feeling not so good about yourself, just remind yourself that you are flawsome."

"Flawsome, what's that?" asked Bianca.

"It means you're still awesome with your flaws and all," said her mom. "Never let anyone take you out of your character and do things you know are not right, and never let anyone make you feel less than. There is only one you, and no one is better at being you than yourself. You are royalty, princess, so always rock your crown."

"But Bianca you have friends of all races and some with long hair, some with short hair, even some with store bought hair." They both chuckled. "So what's so upsetting to you about Jasmine?" asked her mom.

"I don't know," said Bianca. "I guess because she was getting so much attention, I thought my friends would leave me alone to go be her friend."

"Well if that ever happened, they weren't your true friends to begin with," said her mom.

"You're right," said Bianca. "But it was like there was a bad little red angel sitting on one shoulder and the little white angel on the other shoulder, whispering to me what to do. You know, like in the movies," said Bianca. They both laughed. "And the bad angel's stuff just sounded so much better. I guess because I was mad, huh?" asked Bianca. "Yes," said mom.

"But you should always listen to the good angel because it's always the right time to do what's right, no matter how mad you are."

"You can all be friends, and you can still be a leader, but you have to learn to compromise. You should want to see others succeed also and not fail. You must realize you are not going to always win, but instead you just may learn something. Look at it like this, there's no such things as losses, just lessons learned," said her mom.

"Huh?" asked Bianca. "What does that mean?"

"It means there's a lesson to be learned in every situation you come upon, whether you win or lose. So think about what this situation with Jasmine has taught you," her mother said.

"One I can think of right now is to not try and bring others down just to make yourself look or feel better, and learn to share the spotlight sometimes," said Bianca.

"That's what I'm talking about," said her mom. "You should want friends that push you to be greater. Tomorrow is a new day, so we are going to hit the reset button and get off to a fresh start. I think you need to apologize to Jasmine and get to know her for who she really is instead of assuming she's out to get you."

"Oh, mom," said Bianca in a whiny voice.

"Oh, Bianca," said her mom in the same whiny voice.

Just down the street at Jasmine's house, her mom was giving her the same talk. "Jazzy, not everyone is going to always like you, and that's OK as long as you like yourself. Know that you are enough just the way you are. Some people are going to be mean no matter what, but you should continue to treat everyone right because it is the right thing to do. You cannot control how other people feel, but you can control how you respond. You must stop trying to always fit in when you were born to stand out. Real friends will accept you for who you are. You are special, kind, and unique. Never dim your light in order to please people. You are a diamond, so let your light shine."

The next morning Jasmine and her mom pulled up to the school, and who was waiting outside? Bianca. Bianca and her mom waited on the sidewalk as Jasmine and her mom got out of the car. "Hey, Jazz, over here!" yelled Bianca while waving her hand to get her attention.

"Who's that?" asked her mom. "Oh, that's the girl I was arguing with," said Jasmine in a sad voice. They slowly walked toward them. Jasmine's mom reached out her hand to Bianca. "Hi, I'm Jasmine's mom," said Mrs. Green. "You are such a beautiful young girl," she told Bianca. Bianca eyes widened in surprise.

"Really?" asked Bianca in amazement.

"Yes, you are," said Mrs. Green. "And I love your hair. I can never get Jasmine's curls to hold up that tight. Her hair is just too soft."

"Yeah, my curls sometimes fall out before I even get to school," Jasmine said. "I wish I could wear my hair curled the way you do. I especially love it when you have your braids. They look so perfect. I wish I had hair like yours," said Jasmine. Bianca couldn't believe her ears. She instantly thought back to what her mom had said. Bianca never realized that just as bad as she wanted hair and skin like Jasmine's, Jasmine wanted Bianca's hair and skin color.

The girls and their mothers stood outside talking about the conversations they'd had the night before. They explained to the girls, "You both are beautiful. Love the skin you're in."

Then the girls went to the principal's office with their moms. "Well," said Principal Jones, "looks like you two already made up."

"Sure does," said Ms. McClain.

"Yes, we've had a long talk with the girls," said Bianca's mom.

"Well I hope you two learned your lesson and I never have to see you in my office anymore," said Principal Jones.

"We sure did," said Bianca and Jazz, smiling.

"OK, go ahead. Return to class," he said and thanked the moms for coming in.

As the two girls walked into the classroom talking to each other, the others girls' eyes widened from total confusion. "Do you see that?" asked Kim.

"Yeah!" said Kennedi. "I don't know what went on in that office, but I don't think I'm going to like it."

"Listen up, class, Bianca has something she wants to tell you all," said Ms. McClain.

Bianca walked to the front, trembling. "Well I want to apologize to everyone for disrupting the class. I made up stories about Jazz talking about everyone. She never said anything about any of you."

"Aah!" gasped the class.

"I just told you that because I was afraid of losing you guys. I thought you'd no longer want to be my friends, because she was more interesting. I hope you guys aren't mad at me," sniffled Bianca.

"Of course not," said Kennedi.

"Yeah, we totally understand," said Kim and Karly.

Jazz was not upset either. "I probably would have done the same thing if I were in your shoes," said Jazz.

"Nothing or no one can break our bond. We'll always be friends," said the girls.

"Yeah, like Chucky said, 'Friends till the end.' Ha ha ha," laughed Kennedi. The girls apologized to Jazz, and they all hugged it out.

"Oh, that's so sweet," said Benny, pretending to wipe a tear from his eye. "Can I get in on some of the love?" he asked.

"Benny, you are not one of the girls!" yelled Elijah, laughing.

"Yeah, man, get it together," said Adam.

"No, you're not," said Bianca. "But you're one of us, so come on friend."

"Yeah, come on guys. Class hug, class hug," chanted all the girls.

"And you're all invited to my birthday party next week!" yelled out Bianca.

"Hey, party at Bianca's," said Jasmine. "I just hope there's no pin the tail on the donkey," she laughed. As they all hugged it out, Kennedi cried, "Eww, what's that smell?"

"Benny, Berry!" they all yelled and laughed.

"OK, class, this was a valuable lesson that we can all learn from. You should not let jealousy take over your heart. You should not always go off of the words someone else tells you about a person. You should give them a chance and get to know them for yourself. You are all great in your own unique way. You should surround yourself with friends who want to see you grow and bring out the best in you. Remember, there is only one of you, and you can't be replaced."

Jasmine, with a huge smile on her face, thought to herself, "This is going to be one of the best school years after all."

Words to Remember

- You are beautiful, intelligent, and powerful.
- Learn to love who you are, flaws and all.
- There is only one you, and no one can be better at being you than yourself.
- Never compare yourself to others; just focus on being the best version of you.
- You should never feel insecure; everyone is beautiful in their own unique way.
- There's always someone out there looking up to you, and you don't even know it, so always represent yourself well.
- Average effort gives average results, but *extraordinary* effort gives extraordinary results.

- You can do and be whatever you put your mind to.
- You were not born to be average. You were born to *win*!
- You are uniquely made, just the way God wanted you to be.
- You are *that girl*, an original masterpiece, so rock your crown!

This story is about a young girl named Bianca who is used to being the most popular and smartest girl in class. She is everybody's favorite and just loves all the attention. She is a do-it-by-the-book all-around good girl that any parent would love having. Until, one day, a new girl named Jasmine comes to class, and everyone starts showing her all the attention. This does not sit very well with Bianca. Doing everything in her power to destroy the new girl and keep her reigning "queen bee" title, Bianca turns into someone she can't even recognize herself. After things start to really get bad between the girls, Bianca is forced to learn a lesson that all girls should be taught. The story is filled with plot twists that will keep you laughing and surprised throughout the book, and you'll learn the important lesson of self-love and confidence.